W9-CFA-998

LEGO® CITY

ADVENTURES

READY FOR TAKEOFF!

By Sonia Sander
Illustrated by Mada Design

SCHOLASTIC INC.

NEW YORK   TORONTO   LONDON   AUCKLAND

SYDNEY   MEXICO CITY   NEW DELHI   HONG KONG

ISBN 978-0-545-21986-0

20 19   14 15/0

Printed in the U.S.A.   40

First printing, October 2010

LEGO®CITY
AIRLINES

TICKET

GATES
A1-A3
←

GATES
B1-B3
↑

GATES
C1-C3
→

Where is the gate?

It is time to board.
Take out the plane ticket.

AIRPORT

They fill the plane with gas.

The pilot is ready in the cockpit.
The ground crew shows
the pilot where to go.

It is time to fly!
The plane speeds down the runway.
V-r-r-r-o-o-o-m!

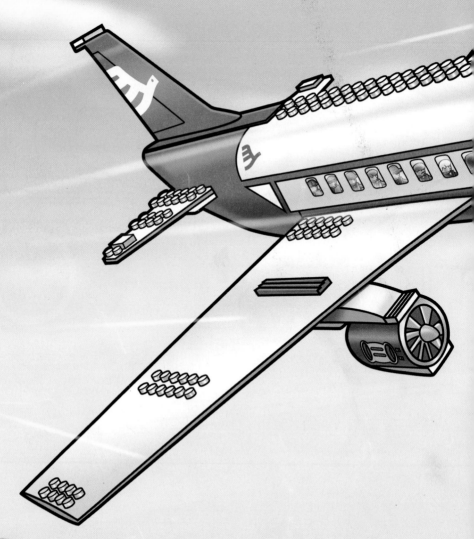

The plane flies into the sky.
It soars above the clouds.

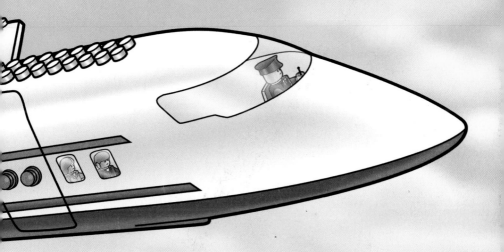

The plane flies a long way.
One last turn before landing.
Down come the wheels.

24

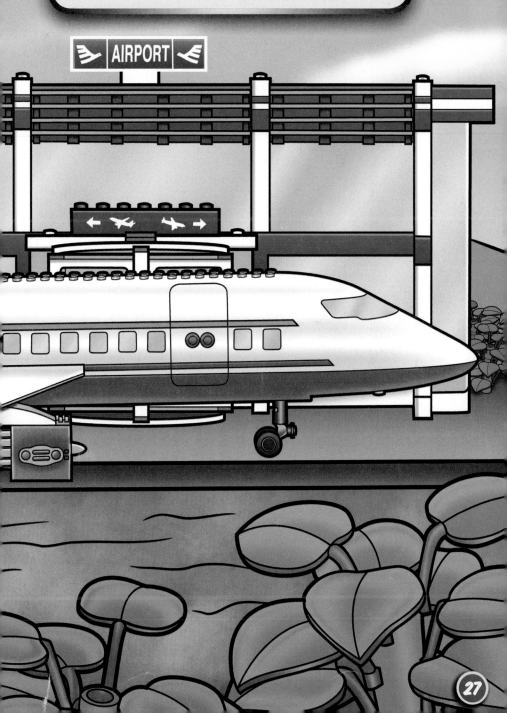

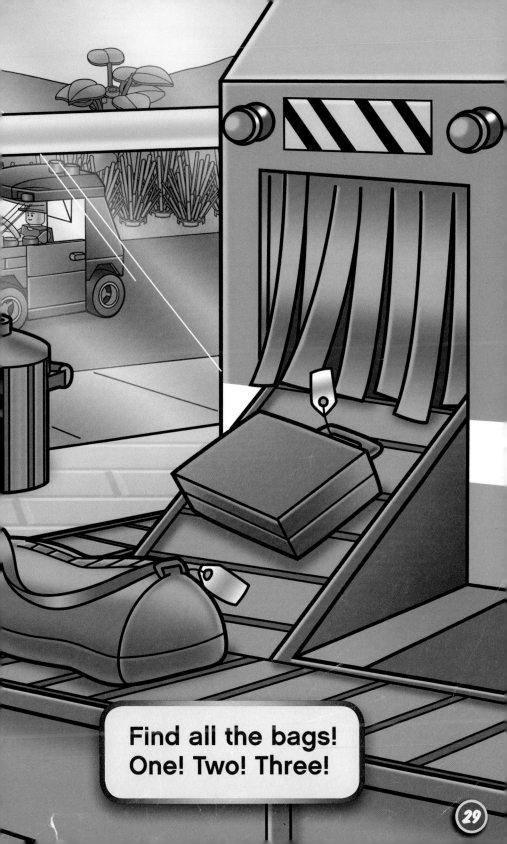

Find all the bags!
One! Two! Three!

BUILD YOUR LEGO LIBRARY!

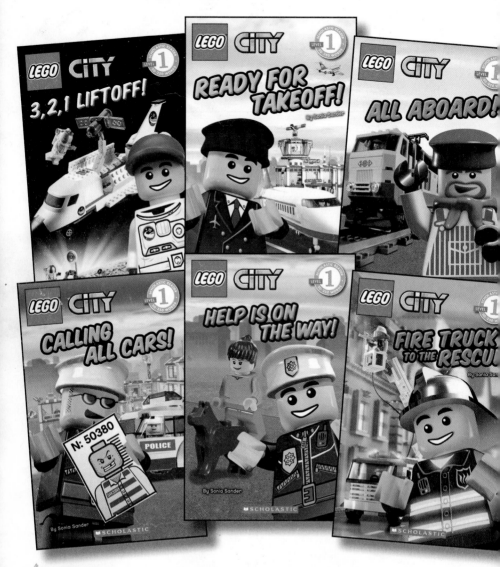

SCHOLASTIC

www.scholastic.com
www.LEGO.com

LEGO